For Dad
P.B.

For Dad
B.C.

First published 2008 by Macmillan Children's Books
This edition published 2009 by Macmillan Children's Books
an imprint of Pan Macmillan.
20 New Wharf Road, London N1 9RR
Associated companies throughout the world
www.panmacmillan.com

ISBN: 978-0-230-70735-1

13 15 14

A CIP catalogue record for this book is available from the British Library.

Printed in China

NOTE TO READERS: The website address
listed in this book is correct at the time of going to print.
However, due to the ever-changing nature of the internet, website addresses and content can change.
The publisher cannot be held responsible for changes in website addresses or content,
or for information obtained through third-party websites.
We strongly advise that all internet searches are supervised by an adult.

Peter Bently

THE SHARK IN THE DARK

Illustrated by Ben Cort

Macmillan Children's Books

Down at the bottom of the deep, dark sea,
Something is stirring and it wants its tea.
His teeth are like knives and his eyes small and beady,
He's big and he's mean and he's terribly greedy.

Watch out, little fishes, watch out for the Shark!
Watch out for the great hungry
Shark in the Dark!

The flounders were floundering.
"Here comes the Shark!"

The turtles were terrified.
"Here comes the Shark!"

"Oh help!" moaned the mackerel.
"The Shark's on his way!
We don't want to be in his belly today!"

And all of the fishes were flustered and bumbling –
"Here comes the Shark and his tummy is rumbling!"

"Now fish," smiled the Shark, "it's been ages since lunch.
I just want a wee fishy something to munch.
Just the tiniest, tastiest, fishiest snack,
So please," grinned the Shark in the Dark . . .

"**...Hey, come back!**"

"No way!" cried the crabs. "We don't mean to sound selfish,
But inside a shark is no place for a shellfish."
"That's right," cried the cod. "We don't want to be tea.
Please go back, Mister Shark, to the dark of the sea!"

"Oh I will," sneered the Shark, "when I've had a few shoals
For my tea. Or fresh lobsters, perhaps? Or some soles?"
And he opened his jaws and his laughter was manic,
And put all the fish in a terrible panic.

Away swam the fish, all desperate to hide
Far from the Shark with his jaws open wide.
"Hello!" said a squid. "What's going on here?
What's all this fussing, what is there to fear?"

"HELP!" flapped the fish. "We're afraid of the Shark,
The big greedy Shark who lives down in the dark.
He's coming to eat us, he's coming right now!
How can we keep him away, tell us, how?"

"I see," frowned the Squid. "So the Shark thinks it's clever
To push you around cos he's bigger than you.
Well, I've got a plan which will make sure he never
Swims this way again. Now, here's what we'll do . . ."

So, along swam the Shark and he peered all around
With his mean, beady eyes – but no fish could be found.
"That's funny," he grumbled. "Where have they all gone?
They can't all have vanished, like that, every one?"

And then, in the distance, he saw a dim shape.
"Aha!" thought the Shark. "THIS small fish won't escape!"

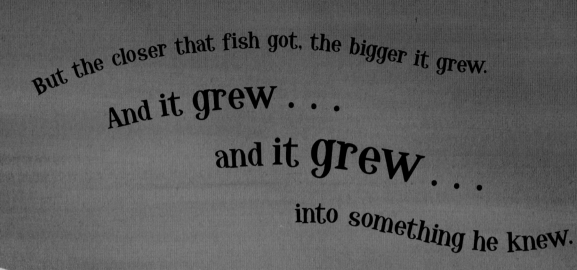

But the closer that fish got, the bigger it grew.

And it grew . . .

and it grew . . .

into something he knew.

The shadowy head
and the shadowy tail,
And the gigantic wide-open jaws of a . . .

. . . WHALE!

"Hey Shark!" boomed the Whale. "Come right here, little fish!
I'm peckish – you're small but you'll do for a dish.
I've come a long way, I need food in my tummy,
A dinner of shark sounds delicious and scrummy!"

With a shiver and shudder the Shark wailed, "Oh heck!
There's no way that I'm going to swim down your neck!"
And then with a flick and a flash of his fin,
The Shark shouted "Bye!" with a half-hearted grin.

And back to the dark fled the Shark in a fright,

As the Whale swam slowly out into the light . . .

"You see," laughed the Squid, "when we all got together,
We taught him a thing he'll remember forever!"